This book belongs to:

....

Sometimes Mimi and her friends fly all the way to our huge world and have lots of fun tiptoeing into toyshops and playing hide-and-seek in the dolls' houses. Before they fly home again, they whisper their stories to Clare and Cally, so now YOU can hear them too!

For all the children and teachers at Meadow Brook Montessori School in Malt Hill. Have fun! - Love C.B.
For Hazel, Chris and Sam with lots of love xx - C.J-I.

Hazel Rose Mimi Acorn Lily

First published 2016 by Macmillan Children's Books
an imprint of Pan Macmillan,
20 New Wharf Road, London N1 9RR
Associated companies throughout the world

www.panmacmillan.com

ISBN: 978-1-4472-9543-3

1 3 5 7 9 8 6 4 2

A CIP catalogue record for this book is available from the British Library.

Printed in China

Mimi's Magical Fairy Friends

Moonbeam the Fairy Dragon

by Clare Bevan and Cally Johnson-Isaacs

MACMILLAN CHILDREN'S BOOKS

FLUTTER! FLURRY! Mimi and her friends couldn't wait to reach the Old Tree House. It was the day of the fairy school outing, and their teacher, Miss Flap, had promised them a big surprise.

“Will we have to fly a long way?” asked Rose.
“Will we need to be brave?” wondered Hazel.
But Miss Flap simply swished her wand and said, “Wait and see!”

Just then, something huge floated past the window
and an elf dressed in starry robes shouted,

"The sky-ship is waiting. Quick flick! Find a seat!
We're sailing away for a magical treat."

The fairies cheered, Miss Flap waved her wand and WHOOSH! everyone was safely inside the wonderful sky-ship.

It flapped its wings with a CLANK and a CLATTER, and away they all soared.

The excited fairies pointed at far-away castles and glittering seas.
"Are we nearly there yet?" they all sang together.

Then down they swooped with a CLANK and a CLANG,
and everyone tumbled out.

"Oh!" cried Mimi joyfully. "It's the Magical Zoo."
"Have a good time," called the elf. "But don't stroke the Green Grump."

"What's a Green Grump?" asked Rose with a shiver.
"Is it big and scary?"

"I hope it's a dragon," said Hazel dreamily. "I love dragons."
Just then, she thought she saw a scaly tail. But when she looked again, it had vanished.

"Here comes the zoo keeper!" shouted Lily.

The zoo keeper was riding the strangest creature the fairies had ever seen. It had a wiggly nose, three humps and a long, twisty tail.

"That isn't a dragon," said Hazel with a sigh.
"Perhaps it's a Green Grump," said Acorn. "Does it bite?"
"No," laughed the zoo keeper, "he's an old Humpty,
and he only bites strawberries."

The zoo keeper jumped down.
"Who wants to see some animals?" she asked.
"WE DO!" shouted the fairies excitedly.

Mimi and her friends had great fun meeting the animals.

The Roundabout Birds raced in circles until everyone felt dizzy,

the Rocking Horses rocked themselves to sleep,

and the Blue Bears were very cuddly.

Even the Green Grump was cute –
but nobody stroked him because he was VERY spiky!

"This is our best school trip ever!" said Mimi.

The zoo keeper clapped her hands. “Follow me to the mini zoo!” In no time, Mimi was stroking an elephant as small as a mouse. Acorn and Lily patted the pocket-sized giraffes while Rose held a tiny cow in her hand.

“I wish I could meet a dragon,” murmured Hazel. Then she blinked. What was that? A scaly nose and bright eyes peeping from behind a tree? But now there was nothing but a buzzing bee.

So Hazel found a quiet corner
and began to sing her secret wish . . .

"Sun and moon and magic zoo,
Make my dragon dreams come true."

The air began to jiggle,
something seemed to spin and . . .

someone else started singing too!
Someone with a tiny, tingly voice.
Suddenly there was a flutter of wings and . . .

FLIP-FLAP-FLOP!

a small, scaly creature flew into Hazel's arms.
"Oh!" she gasped. "My very own dream-dragon."

SWISH! The little dragon tucked his head under his wings. Hazel laughed.

"I saw your nose and your tail and your sparkly eyes. You like playing hide-and-seek, don't you? So do I."

For the rest of the day, Hazel and her mini dragon explored the zoo together and shared a delicious picnic too.

Hazel ate fairy cakes – and the dragon chewed the shiny wrappers.

Then they played hide-and-seek until Miss Flap called,
"Time to go home!" The sky-ship was waiting.

All the fairies found their seats. Except for Hazel. Where had her dragon gone? She waved and she called, but it was no use.

The ship was ready to sail and there was nothing she could do.

"We must hurry," warned the elf. "A cloudy night means no stars and no moon." So they whizzed away quickly.

Poor Hazel. She hadn't even said goodbye to her dragon.

It wasn't long before lightning flashed
and a wild wind blew the ship up and down.

They flew high and low, this way and that way.

Then the sun sank down and the darkness grew.

“I’m sorry,” said the elf. “I’m afraid we’re lost.”
“This is much worse than the Green Grump,” wailed Rose.
“Perhaps we’ll be lost for ever,” said Acorn tearfully.

But Hazel was gazing at a silver glow in the night sky . . .

“My dragon!” cried Hazel. “You found me.”

At once, he stretched his claws, flapped his wings
and opened his mouth wide.
SHIMMER! GLIMMER! GLOW!

A glittering pathway of light appeared and led the ship out of the clouds to a clear sky. "Hooray for Hazel and her magical dragon!" shouted the fairies.

The moon was shining like silver. Hazel hugged her pet dragon. "You are as bright as moonlight," she said proudly. "I know just what to call you . . ."

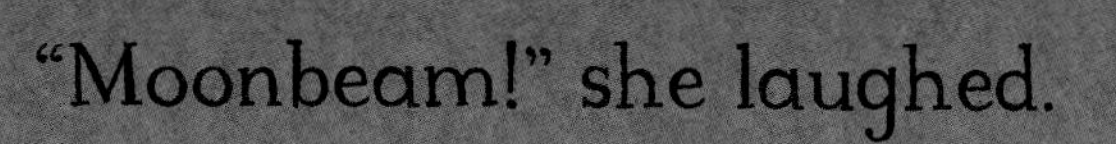

"Moonbeam!" she laughed.

Hazel held him close and the
happy dragon gave a big, sparkly YAWN!

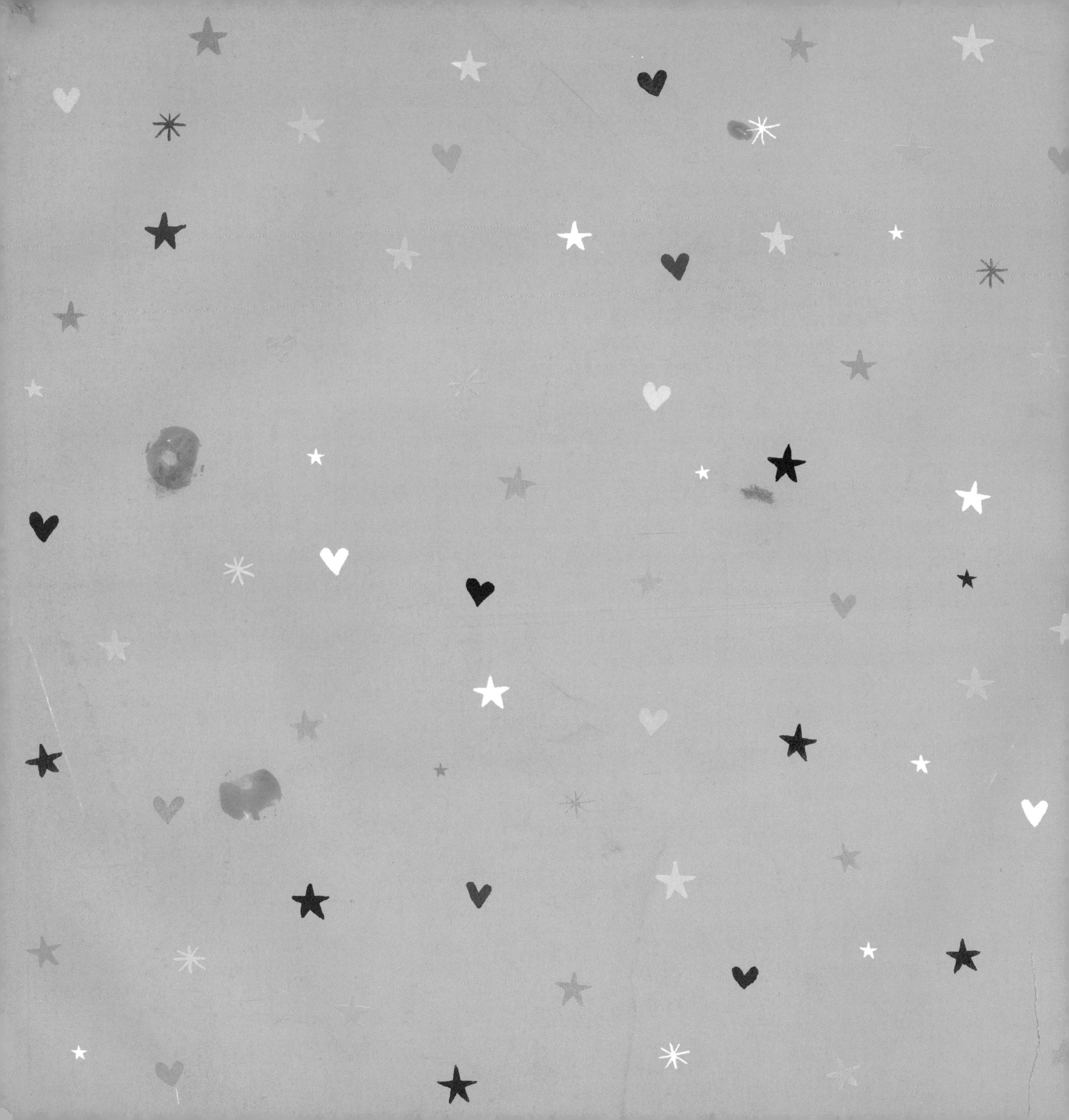